For my family, who always
protect me from the dark ~ SS

For Winston, my dear one.
Also for Dave, Lou (much missed),
Alan and Jennifer ~ LF

LiTTLE TiGER

LONDON

CATERPILLAR BOOKS
An imprint of the Little Tiger Group
www.littletiger.co.uk
1 Coda Studios, 189 Munster Road, London SW6 6AW
First published in Great Britain 2020
Created by Sarah Shaffi • Text by Isabel Otter
Text copyright © Caterpillar Books Ltd 2020
Illustrations copyright © Lucy Farfort 2020
A CIP catalogue record for this book is available from the British Library
All rights reserved • Printed in China
ISBN: 978-1-83891-169-0
CPB/1400/1430/0620
2 4 6 8 10 9 7 5 3 1

AFRAID
of the
DARK

Sarah Shaffi
& Isabel Otter

Illustrated by
Lucy Farfort

Today we are
moving house.

Me, Dad and
our dog, Pickle.

I'm not sure
if I'm ready for
a **new start**.

"Welcome to your new home, Amy," says Dad.
"I think we're going to love it here!"
But Pickle and I are still not sure.

It doesn't **feel** like
home yet.

My new room is **strange** and **scary**.

I think I can see shadowy monsters lurking in dark corners... and what's that

tap - tap - tapping

at the window?

How will I
ever get to
sleep?

It's morning and the shadow monsters have crawled away but I don't feel very well.

Dad is making pancakes with maple syrup.
"Shall we go to the library later?" he asks.

I want to go, but I'm still feeling a bit funny.

Dad can always tell when something is wrong.
"Don't worry, Amy. This will soon feel like home," he whispers.

The library has more books
than I have ever seen.
The shelves go on and on!

"What sort of books are you
looking for?" asks a kind voice.

I feel a bit shy but I
say that I like stories
with magic in them.

"I see," says
the library lady.

"Wonderful tales of adventure that will carry
you to far-away lands. I know just the thing…"

When Dad reads me
the story I really do travel
into a land of adventure.

I know the shadow
monsters are hiding
somewhere but with
Dad there they don't
come too close.

But the story
doesn't work.

As soon
as Dad
tiptoes out,

the

monsters

come

back.

In the morning, I play with my animals and forget
all about the horrible shadow monsters.
Pickle likes to play too!

Are those voices coming from outside?

I can just see out
of the window if I go
on my tippy-toes.

There are
children
waving at
me!

The children are playing
in a den but the tunnel looks
a bit dark and shadowy.

A smiley face pops out.
"Come and play with us! You can
get through the gap in the fence."

Before I can speak, Pickle starts trotting towards the den.
I can't let him go alone.

Inside, it isn't dark and scary at all!

"I'm Sofia and this is Bilal. Welcome to our secret den!"

I hear Dad calling and we run
back to the house. For the first time
since the big move, I feel like
I'm **going home**.

Dad has a special surprise
planned for tonight...

He tells me a story.

"There was once a little girl who was very afraid of the dark. She wished she could make a cloak out of stars to drive the shadows away.

Then, one night, Amy realised that her cloak of stars had been there all along, she just had to look up."

The little girl is me!

Dad and I hang
stars in my bedroom.

It doesn't feel
strange and scary
any more.

It feels **magical!**

The shadow
monsters are gone at last.

I fall asleep straight away,
safe under my **cloak of stars**.